The Last Day of Marcus Tullius Cicero

THE LAST DAY OF MARCUS TULLIUS CICERO

a novella

JORDAN M. POSS

Quotation from Cicero's *Tusculan Disputations* from the translation by Andrew P.
Peabody (Boston: Little, Brown, 1886)
Quotation from Cicero's *Tenth Philippic* by Tom Holland from *Rubicon: The Last Years
of the Roman Republic* (New York: Anchor, 2003)
Quotation from Plutarch's *Cicero* from the translation by Rex Warner in *The Fall of the
Roman Republic* (Harmondsworth: Penguin Classics, 1958)

Set in 12 pt. Monotype Fournier Std.
Map by Jordan Poss
Author photograph by Scott Poss

for Sophie, my Tullia

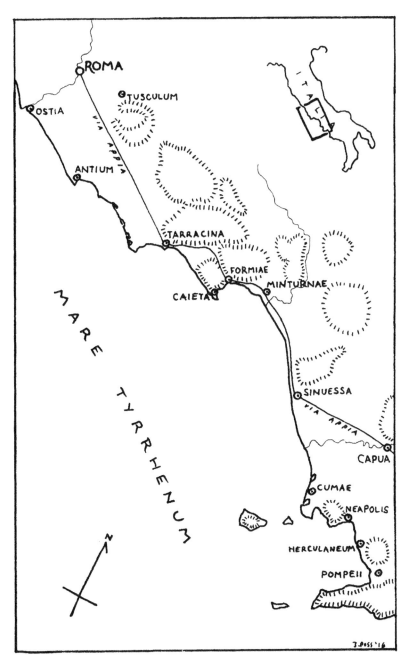

Italy at the time of Cicero's flight, November–December 43 BC

THE LAST DAY OF MARCUS TULLIUS CICERO

[7 December 43 BC]

Gladiators, too . . . what do they endure! How much rather will those who have been well trained receive a wound than avoid it by any show of cowardice! . . . What gladiator of moderate reputation ever groaned, or lost countenance, or showed himself a coward as he stood in combat, or even as he lay down to die? Or what one of them, when he had lain down and was ordered to receive the fatal stroke, ever drew his neck back? So much can exercise, habit, and thought avail.

—Cicero, *Tusculan Disputations*

So glorious is it to recover liberty, that it is better to die than shrink from regaining it.

—Cicero, *Tenth Philippic*

WE HAD SAILED THROUGH THE NIGHT FROM ANTIUM, and Marcus Tullius came on deck at daybreak, as we neared Caieta. One would not have known he was on the run. He was a magnificent man even in old age, even as his body failed him. His oratorical postures are well known; even his silences are famous to this day—left elbow cocked on the arm of a chair, the chin at rest in the upturned palm, and the lips and great crest of nose turned in damning boredom upon the subject of his gaze. Such he could still do, as well as strut and gesture and slice the air with one hand freed of his toga, but other things had begun to fail. Though he would not, in his vanity, let on, his eyes were not as sharp as in the past. One hip troubled him, depending on the weather, and he relied upon our sedan chair rather more often than he had used to. The middle finger of his right hand had begun to seize, to lock in place. He would pop it back into motion with great effort and an alarming crack, and after a time of writing or of holding some utensil, it would have seized again into place, now as a talon hooked around the stylus. Small things, but things we slaves did not miss, even if the old man could deceive the Senate and the people.

And that morning, he did look old. He had not washed or shaved for a few days, since turning back on the road to Rome. One would have thought he was in mourning. His face was drawn and pale, and his hair unkempt and longer than was his wont. He had risen from a camp bed below and looked like an old centurion, past due for retirement but refusing to leave his legion, even as senescence overtook him.

He stood and watched the sailors furl the sail as we approached the headland and sunlight first touched the heights. He saw me after a moment and greeted me.

"Good morning, Leonidas."

"And to you, master."

He hobbled across the deck—I learnt later that he had never gotten his sea legs, and the old Romans loved him for it—and stretched.

"Not far now."

"No, sir."

I took a closer look at him. "Are you well?"

He nodded rather too vigorously. "Quite," he said. And

after a moment, "Seasickness."

"Yes, sir." We had had a rough night sailing from Antium—a December storm blew in and had threatened to dash us on the coast.

"I asked the captain to put in near Caieta. I can go no farther like this. We will stay a while at the villa there before moving on."

I doubted the wisdom of halting—again—while Marcus Antonius's henchmen were a threat, but nodded and pointed forward to the left, to the headland sheltering the entrance to the bay at Formiae. He looked. Golden morning light crept down a high temple. The wooded shore soughed in the breeze, tossing not unlike the sea itself in the dawn's last gloaming.

"Ah!" he said after a time. His eyes, you remember. "Apollo's temple. Donated something to it myself a while back, you know."

"Yes, master," I said. We all knew.

He looked up at the morning sky, a sweep of pearl, gold, and every shade of azure.

"Appropriate sight first thing in the morning, is it not?"

"Sir?"

He gestured, and I marked the finger crooked down into the palm as he pointed to the temple. "The first rays of the sun

3

blessing a shrine to Apollo."

"Ah," I said in my turn.

He shrugged. "Divine coincidence everywhere, I suppose. You will ask for news of Quintus when we have arrived?"

"Yes, sir." My master had parted ways with his brother some days before, Quintus—poor, despairing Quintus—having decided to hang back. He had taken nothing when he had fled his home, and so had had nothing with which to sustain his flight. The brothers would seek their Fortunes separately. One prayed, as we all did, that Quintus Tullius Cicero might be spared—it was Marcus Tullius Cicero that Marcus Antonius wanted dead.

He nodded and took his right hand in his left and then gave me a shifty glance. I pretended not to notice, and with a cruel jerk he snapped his finger straight out again. He shook the hand a few times as if fanning himself.

"Unseasonably warm," he said.

I suppressed a laugh. "Yes, sir," I said. It was for a December morning on the sea.

The sailors had run out the oars and rowed now, bringing us around the headland and into the harbor, heading for shore.

Others came on deck. A handful of slaves, my master's freedman secretary, Tiro, in his cap, a bodyguard in an army

4

cloak. I had spoken to him a few times—he was called Gnaeus Mucius but came from a small and unstoried side of that clan. He had spent nineteen years in the army and served in every capacity available. He had been a senior centurion with Pompeius the Great at his defeat in Greece and come home with Julius Caesar's pardon—like Brutus and Cassius. He had hoped for retirement to a country farm and a bosomy Samnite girl but, no sooner had Caesar been murdered, he saw new threats to the Republic and offered his services to my master, who quietly accepted.

"Good morning, Senator," Gnaeus said as he stepped on deck. He walked crab-wise to the gunwale and leaned against it. Another old Roman meant to walk terra firma, not sail the seas like a Greek.

He nodded to me, said "Greekling," and grinned. This was our joke—I am not Greek but Thracian by blood; I received the name Leonidas as a young slave in another household.

"A good morning, recruit." This was my joke.

"It is, and the same to you."

As we rounded the spit of rock guardingCaieta from the sea, Tiro came alongside us and nodded to the temple, yawing ever nearer above the waves. "A beautiful sight to redeem a night spent retching overboard," he said. Tiro, like our master, had a way with words. You will have read his finer accounts of what I will relate.

"A temple to Apollo," I said.

"Yes, I've been to this estate before."

"Your expertise, as always, is appreciated," Gnaeus said.

"I have been to this estate too, you know."

Tiro gave me a look. We had known each other for years. I knew he did not appreciate tweaking, and he knew why I was anxious to land and reach the villa.

Tiro itched under his freedman's cap and began to speak, but was interrupted. A sharp noise came to us from the direction of the shore, like scornful, nasal laughter. We turned and looked again. There seemed to be smoke coming from the temple. It rose in wisps that rapidly twisted and curled back on themselves. There was something uncanny about the movement of this smoke.

"That's some wind," one of the sailors said.

"Morning sacrifice?" my master said.

"Not their usual schedule," Tiro said.

"And what is that damned noise?" Gnaeus said.

We stared, each of us attempting to unriddle the nature of this smoke. I saw my master put the ball of his fist into his hip and hoist himself forward, squinting toward the temple.

Perhaps his sight had not deteriorated to the point I had thought, because I believe to this day that I heard him say:

"Crows?"

Suddenly, the smoke dissolved and whipped downward from the temple to the sea, and a flight of great black crows overtook our ship and whirled about us, cawing and batting their wings at us like the harpies. One of the sailors screamed and ducked into the cover of the sail. The rest of us crouched and covered our heads—all except my master. He stood in his old way—unstooped, head raised, hands poised to strike at the audience—but with a look of uttermost resignation upon his face.

At last the crows checked their flight and landed in great numbers all over the ship—the yardarm and gunwales were lined with them, and they busily cawed at us, cocked their sharp black eyes at us, and pecked and nibbled the ropes.

"Shoo, you," Gnaeus said, and swatted at them with his centurion's staff. "Get on, damn you."

The sailor beneath the sail peeked out, trembling, and ducked back under the sailcloth when he saw.

My master approached him. "What troubles you?"

The sailor presented only a trembling hand and pointed. "These crows, sir."

7

The captain of the ship, an old Neapolitan, bearded like Neptune himself, called from the rear of the ship: "A bad omen, Senator."

He need not have explained—we were all familiar with the augur's art, divining the flight of birds. I turned to look at my master. This was his moment. He loved to dispense wisdom, to dredge up some ancient saying or thought of his own that would bring light to a dark time. We slaves sometimes received these wisdoms too often—he once held forth to me for an hour on old Cato's advice regarding farming, with his own glosses, while I redug a drainage ditch in his garden on a hot day—but we did not despise him for it. When his wisdom came at the right time, it was exactly the right time.

I awaited his speech—some surprising moral to be drawn from the moment—but none came. It shocked me as much as his calm in the middle of the crows did, but Marcus Tullius Cicero nodded, bit his lip as if in thought, and said nothing more until we came to shore.

*

WE HOVE TO IN A QUIET COVE BETWEEN CAIETA AND Formiae, and set about preparing to carry the household to

Marcus Tullius's villa inland between the two towns. The sailors dragged the ship prow-first onto the beach until it was stable, and then assisted the household slaves and freedmen in unloading my master's cargo. There was no great deal, just enough to delay us on the strand for an hour or so. In addition to the letters, books, notes, wax tablets, and surplus writing materials—all in watertight cases of Tiro's design—we had the sedan chair and an assortment of carrying poles depending on the manpower available for lifting it, a lot of food and provisions and two amphorae of imported wine my master could not leave his estate in Tusculum without. This may sound like luxury, but for a man of a long and prestigious career, widely published and a great authority, Marcus Tullius traveled light into exile. After all, he had done it before.

As we unloaded and then arranged the goods for travel to the villa, he stood on the shore carrying the one item he would not leave to the slaves to move—a small painted figurine out of the household shrine in Tusculum, a figurine of Tullia.

Gnaeus fell to and directed our work. A centurion never really retires. Throughout, he never strayed more than a few steps from my master. Tiro moved to and fro accounting for the handful of goods and making certain the sailors did not break or steal anything. I liked Tiro. He was fussy and wore his learning on his sleeve—what poor boy made good does not?—but he was kind and had not fallen into the trap awaiting most former slaves, of cruelty to those yet in servitude. But most importantly, he was faithful. He had returned from the farm for which he had toiled and scrimped as a freedman to help our master in his time of need.

The sailors and some of the slaves murmured darkly about the crows as we worked. We had all seen bird-sign a thousand thousand times. My master would have seen the skies read for flight—sometimes multiple times—before every meeting of the Senate. But here there was dispute about what the omen meant. I wearied of the talk. In the absence of a trained augur, everyone is an expert. I worked as quickly as I could, ignoring the murmurs, so that we could pack up and head to the villa. I wanted to see Clementia.

Clementia—it was not her real name, which was some unpronounceable German noise, but it suited her well. We had met some years ago during a summer retreat to the coast, where the sea breezes and the height above the shore kept the villa cool. She was a young thing, newly purchased in Mediolanum, and I not much older. I was under Tiro's tutelage at the time, preparing to be one of his potential replacements upon his manumission, and the mistress put Clementia to work in the gardens during the day and putting the final touches on dinner in the evenings. We fell for each other, and ended the weeks of that summer fumbling about with each other as often as possible in the concealment of a shaded lane nearby, invisible from the house above. Every summer since had been the same.

I looked at Tiro scraping notes into a wax tablet on the shore, at my master's side. Those years ago, when I met Clementia, the possibility seemed so remote as not to warrant thought, but now I hoped. I prayed for manumission, for my master to make me a free man. I had saved what I could. The first thing I would do is redeem Clementia, marry her, and use what little we had left to settle on a farm in the hills. Tiro had done it through faithful service. I had spent the eleven years in the household trying to do the same.

But for now, there was the reunion with Clementia.

At last, the sun was well up over the hills and shining down on the shore, and the naked sailors pulled on their tunics and headed to town for wine and whoring. Tiro took a final look at the goods and nodded. He turned to Marcus Tullius.

My master did not immediately react. I looked closely. He was lost in thought—uncharacteristically so. Tiro cleared his throat, and my master looked up.

"All is ashore and ready?" he said.

"Yes, sir."

"Thank you, Marcus Tiro. I am ready myself, and as heavy a load as anything else on this beach."

We laughed and eight of us bore him up in the sedan chair for the walk to the villa.

Even with the extra numbers the walk was hard. We went mostly uphill in the rugged coastal terrain, avoiding the main roads and taking smaller, broken tracks to avoid detection. And with his joint aches, my master had put on weight in the last year or two, and he had never been lean, like the late Julius Caesar, or outright scrawny, like the late lamented Cato. I had volunteered to help lift, though technically that was beneath my station, and had the pole at his right, immediately behind the chair. I tried to get a glimpse of him. His color looked better now that he was ashore, but there was still something corpse-like about him. I supposed that had become normal. He had never been quite the same since Tullia died.

It was the well past the third hour of the day by the time we caught sight of the villa, reared above the path on a rocky outcropping. This villa was unique among my master's holdings in two particulars—it was smaller than had become usual among the senatorial class in Rome, and it was older than any other house my master owned. When my master's old enemy Clodius Pulcher—an impious demagogue my master had once testified against on a charge of incest—had forced him into exile, he had had the state confiscate and burn every house his men could get hold of. Clodius had even erected a temple on the ruins of my master's house in Rome, to further complicate his efforts to get his property back should he ever return. The only house Clodius's men had not gotten to was this one, set in the rough, secluded hill country about a mile from the sea. The house represented, as few things could, a time before the last ten years of trouble. With it in sight, my heart and my step quickened. A few times the men ahead of me grunted a curse, told me to slow down and keep pace.

"Now, now, Leonidas, the girl is still there," Marcus Tullius said. I flushed.

"Of course, sir."

I sensed rather than saw him smile. "Self-control will get you what you want, and allow you to keep it, too."

I felt heartened. I ache to think back on it. "Yes, sir."

I felt him sit up and he called out, "Quicken the pace, lads, we are all weary."

We made the hill and were setting the chair down at the door of the house in minutes. I fought to keep my composure as we waited.

13

Tiro opened the door and Marcus Tullius, with Gnaeus just ahead of him, stepped into the house. I wiped my brow and nodded to the other panting bearers and followed.

In the entryway, my master placed the figurine of Tullia on the shelf above the household altar. He then went servant by servant, greeting them. He moved slowly, and concealed it by lingering over his greetings. But I marked the way he rubbed his hip under the folds of his toga. Gnaeus hung back by the altar, eyeing the line of slaves. He had both hands under his cloak, ready to defend my master if necessary. I had seen the look in his eye and that dangerous posturemany times before in Caesar. But here the aggression was directed toward protecting an old man, not bringing down an old republic.

I searched the room for Clementia. At last, I saw her, down at the end of the line beyond our master, obscured from sight by his hunched bulk. She caught my eye and suppressed a grin—I could see it in the way she pursed her lips, and the tip of her nose dipped inward with the strain.

"Ah, Clementia," my master said, shifting ungracefully to her. "Dear Clementia, how is your Latin?"

She said something demurely low, but I caught a sharp sound or two—verbal relics of her childhood beyond the Rhine. Her eyes ticked from him to me and back.

14

"I look forward to some of that fish sauce you have perfected," he was saying. "You have surpassed them all, dear Clementia. Now——" he said, with a clap of his hands. He struck one of his rostrum-appropriate poses, and said to the assembled household, "To your work. Waste no more time on account of an old Senator."

The servants scattered. My master, with three or four others, headed into the house toward the inner courtyard and its garden. I started for Clementia, but she gave me a look that stopped me.

"Clementia?"

She did not move from her place, but jerked her head after our master. "Go to him."

"I—"

"Go."

She looked divine, if it is not sacrilege to say so. The poets do. Her hair was still white-blonde, her eyes the unnatural blue of those marshland barbarians. She had filled out since last I saw her, and looked the better for it. My confusion vied with my eyes, which searched the folds of her clothing for her shape.

She noticed and looked away. Finally, she raised a hand, and motioned again after Marcus Tullius. "Later. Now go."

I nodded, watched her go, and then followed my master

deeper into the house.

I caught up in the courtyard. My master lowered himself with a hint of difficulty to the low wall around the garden. Gnaeus stepped forward to assist, but hesitated and hung back. Tiro stood busy with his wax tablet beside three others— Spintharus, formerly one of Tiro's replacements as secretary but now freeman butler of this house, the captain of the ship, and a wizened old man in a senatorial toga, whom I did not recognize. I stepped up as the old man greeted my master in the elaborate but out-of-date fashion of the ancient clients— solicitous but not giddy, deferential without servility, anxious to please without toadying—a way that seemed to honor both men at the same time.

My master glanced at me and bade the old man pause with a gesture.

"Ah, Leonidas. 'Give your ship over to the winds, but never your soul to a woman,' Leonidas."

I could not help but laugh. "That's good, sir. Yours?"

"My brother's. Speaking from experience."

"Your brother was not so fortunate as you were, sir." Tiro glanced at me. Our master's two marriages were a touchy subject, especially the second, not long dissolved.

"Our fortunes were similar, but no—he did not bear it as he

ought." I was relieved, until he sat up with a jerk and looked me in the eye. "Any news of Quintus?"

I had forgotten. "I will inquire, sir. I apologize—"

He waved me off. "No need for that. We have yet time."

I nodded and caught a glimpse of Clementia, bustling past an open door across the courtyard. In elder days the garden had been one of her responsibilities; it looked as though she still kept it up. This being December, little grew and nothing bloomed, but its cultivation was lovely and our master enjoyed greeting visitors here or reading when the light in his library failed.

I watched her go as he turned again to the old senator.

"No need as well for the elaborate greeting, Germanicus. My friends, you know or surely know of Caius Quinctilius Falx Germanicus, late of the Senate, one-time Censor, and now enjoying retirement and the waters of Formiae?"

We greeted him as was appropriate to our differing stations. I recognized the name—he had won some relatively minor engagement against Clementia's people and thus earned his honorific—but that had been long ago. I looked more closely as Marcus Tullius introduced us. The man was not merely wizened but withered, a husk, wrinkled like the sand at low tide from hairless head to crooked toe. The dignity and glory of his feats were long ago, well before this time of trouble.

"Germanicus has brought news from Rome."

"Eh, gossip more like," Germanicus said. "But it comes from persons I trust."

"Yes?"

"Marcus Antonius is another Sulla. He has taken the proscriptions in earnest, and Caesar—or that boy called Caesar—is reconciled to his partner's murders."

Sulla's proscriptions, his hit list of enemies, was a nightmare memory of the older men of the Republic. The late Caesar had lived through it as a youth; the late Pompeius had gotten his start in the butchery. My master listened grimly. "Go on."

"You know the tribune, Salvius?"

"Yes."

"When he heard for certain that his name was on the lists that Caesar, Antonius, and Lepidus had agreed upon, he gave a feast to bid his friends farewell before going into exile. One of Antonius's men caught up to him during the feast and, with the tables laden and all of Salvius's guests reclining, hauled Salvius down over the table by the hair and hacked his head off. Carried it right out and left everyone reclining at a bloody table, his corpse still twitching on the floor."

"Yes."

"Another they cornered in the Forum during an assembly. He ducked into a shop and changed clothes, but his retinue hung around out of pity and got him recognized and killed. Another, Annalis, was abandoned by his retinue and killed without a fight."

I looked at Gnaeus. He leaned, his eyes to the ground and inscrutable, against a pillar, and listened.

"Antonius's men caught up to Turranius and he requested a stay of execution until his son—you know the effeminate wastrel, he runs in Antonius's circles—could make a plea on his behalf to Antonius. The soldiers laughed and said—" Germanicus choked. "Do you know what they said to him? 'He already has, but to the opposite effect.' That's what this republic has come to, Marcus Tullius. Sons handing their fathers over to destruction. Everything is upside—"

My master raised a hand, and Germanicus stopped. My master sat now with his face in his hands.

After a long time, he muttered, "I am fortunate I had the wisdom to send young Marcus out of the country." He raised his head and composed himself. "Not out of any fear of him on my part, you understand, but fear for him. I will be no Turranius, I am sure, but neither do I want to lose—another child."

"Fathers and sons are being slain together, as will no doubt not surprise you," Germanicus said.

"Nothing can surprise me anymore. But enough. What did you say of Caesar?"

"He takes no action to stop Antonius. You can count on no help from him."

"You are sure?"

"I am sure. They have an agreement. Antonius is the more powerful man—Caesar's lieutenant! What is a twenty-year old adopted son to do in the face of the deified Gaius Julius Caesar's most trusted man? Antonius has the upper hand. You should depart at once for Greece. Junius Brutus will much appreciate your presence in his army—it will lend him the legitimacy of the Senate."

"I have considered it, yes." My master had considered everything. He had at first made for Greece, as Germanicus was suggesting anew, and even turned back toward Rome at one point. The situation was unclear. We wandered in a fog from villa to villa. "Gnaeus Mucius," he said at last.

Gnaeus straightened. "Yes, sir."

"You know Caesar—or know his reputation?"

"I knew Julius Caesar, Senator, and have met the young Caesar."

"And what is your estimation of him?"

"Like the Senator, he comes from humble origins."

"Comparison is unflattering in this situation, centurion."

"You misunderstand me, Senator. I mean—" Gnaeus was no Cicero. This could take some time. "With respect, he has heart, but is a youth, and is untried. Marcus Antonius is tried."

"Thank you, Gnaeus Mucius."

"Sir."

My master raised his left hand to his chin and touched it, thinking. Germanicus waited.

"You know, Germanicus," my master said at length, "I had half-considered taking Cato's way out, but doing him one better. I would travel to Rome, to Antonius's house, and kill myself on his hearth." Germanicus's eyes widened. The action was rash—suicide was just becoming fashionable then—but it would have brought a curse into Antonius's household. The goddess of the hearth would have forsaken him, and the spirits of his ancestors would have fled. Antonius's family would drift lifeless, with no guide or purpose. It would have been vengeance for my master, yes, but at an unthinkable price.

"Marcus—to think a few insults to Antonius and his wife, a few speeches against him in the Senate—"

"Speeches! Someone has to speak. Brutus and his ilk,

murderers all, but at least they did away with a king. They struck for liberty, but they forgot this one thing—you do not kill tyranny by killing a tyrant. Marcus Antonius took Caesar's place within a week. He is as much a threat as his old master was. I had thought we had a friend in this, but now the son, the boy Caesar, after so many overtures of peace and of the rule of law, after so many assurances to my face, has caved in. Handed us name by name on a list to that bull-necked pederast. No. Speaking was the least I could do, just one more service to my country in a long career of service. We did not build this republic to succumb to a strong man."

"The people, Marcus," Germanicus said. "Caesar was ever the favorite of the people."

"Damn the people," my master said.

"The best men then? The aristocracy?"

"Damn them. Damn them both."

There was a silence. Tiro shifted his weight. I found I was holding my breath.

At last, Gnaeus said, "At least you are at the top of Antonius's list. That's some kind of flattery."

My master immediately burst into laughter. He rose with no difficulty, walked to Gnaeus and clapped him on the shoulder. Gnaeus grinned. My master turned back to Germanicus, beaming.

"Come come, you should stay for lunch. We can talk more afterward. Perhaps go for a walk."

Germanicus still looked uncomfortable. "I am not much for walking these days, and, if you do not mind my saying so—"

"I am getting old, too, yes. I have actually written a book on the subject. Have you read it?"

I looked at Tiro. We both grinned. Germanicus goggled at our master. He could barely keep up. Few could.

"Book? No, I—I believe not."

"Tiro, have a copy sent round to Germanicus. I dedicated the book to my dear friend Atticus—we are both growing so old!—but perhaps you, Germanicus, would have been the better dedicatee."

He led Germanicus away from the garden. The offer of lunch was not really optional. As he went, I caught Gnaeus's eye. The soldierly bluff he had shown in joking, blunting the edge of the moment, had gone. He seemed burdened, as I felt burdened. Tiro showed it too. When the two elders had gone, we followed.

Ahead, my master ambled toward the dining room. His limp returned bit by bit as he walked and, as he showed Germanicus through the door, I saw him turn, his body blocking the view, and pull at the seizing finger of his right hand.

*

WITH MARCUS TULLIUS, GNAEUS, TIRO, AND GERMANICUS
reclining for the midday meal, I struck out to discover
something of Quintus. My master's brother was just as vain as
he, but more temperamental, more prone to panic or brood, and
therefore more prone to send letters or a messenger at the first
sign of trouble. We should have heard something of him. I did
not expect what we would hear.

I questioned Spintharus outside the dining room. He
assured me there had been no word from Quintus Tullius for
some time. "I am unsurprised," he said. "Marcus Tullius did
arrive somewhat unexpectedly, after all. We had barely any
time at all to prepare for his arrival."

"You have performed magnificently nonetheless," I said,
and turned to go.

Spintharus caught me lightly by the shoulder. "Leonidas—
I wonder, how long does he plan to stay?"

"You know as much as I do," I said. "He was talking of
Greece earlier. And the army of Junius Brutus."

"Yes, and he's sent young Marcus on ahead."

I waited. Spintharus thought for a while. Quite a while. He

24

was a good thinker, Spintharus, but slow. He had required precise, deliberate dictation when still serving as secretary, and so was soon relegated to specialized work. He was an excellent one for mulling the precise word one wanted, but not who you wanted for shorthand transcripts of public speeches.

At last, I offered: "I suspect a day or two here, and then onward, Spintharus."

"Greece?"

I shrugged.

"You don't think he'd return to Rome? Go to Antonius's house—he said—"

"No, our master is no Cato." Oh, Marcus Porcius Cato, the last of the Old Romans. None could match your virtue or your stoicism. Besieged by Julius Caesar in Utica, and unwilling to give Caesar the pleasure of pardoning him or of witnessing the descent of the Republic into tyranny, Cato gutted himself one evening after dinner. His slaves discovered him and tried to bind his wound, but no sooner had he recovered consciousness than he ripped out their stitches and finished by hand what he had started with his sword. I had no doubt my master was brave, but his stoicism would not lead to self-murder, I felt sure.

"No, there was only one Cato," Spintharus said, and shuddered. I half-turned to go again, when he said, not really to me or to anyone, "A remarkable world this has become. To be arrayed against a Caesar is to will your own death. To make peace with a Caesar is to be consigned to destruction."

I shuddered myself. The notion of fate had not crossed my mind before, but it looked as though the Caesars were fated to sweep all away before them. They did claim descent from Venus, after all, and now Julius Caesar's son was putting it about that his father had taken a place among the gods. But then, the gods had to answer to Fate as well.

I bade Spintharus farewell and started for my master's office. I meant to check for unopened, unread letters, things the well-meaning Spintharus may have missed. I came out of the entry hall into the courtyard and ran into Clementia. I forgot all about the letters.

"Clementia—"

She whispered, "Come, Leonidas," and led me by the hand through the little enclosed garden, into a guest suite, and out a side door into a shady spot overlooking the distant sea. We had met often at this spot as a prelude to walking, arm in arm, down to that tree-lined lane below the hill. In the summer flowers grew here, but today there stood only stubble. The sun had just passed its zenith and the land began to come into relief again; the trees on the shore cast stunted shadows and the rocky swales of the land between were becoming sun-rounded again. Far, far off, I caught sight of the temple on the promontory above Caieta. I thought of the crows again just before Clementia spoke.

"Leonidas, forgive me."

I looked at her. Tears stood in her eyes. "Forgive you?"

"For your reception this morning. Our master's arrival—everything has been upset. In an uproar."

"He's in great danger, Clementia, and we have duties to perform."

She laughed once and wiped one eye. "He would be so proud to hear you talk like that."

"I mean there is nothing to forgive. And I am glad to see you now."

"And I you, Leonidas." She kissed me, and I put my arm about her. She pressed close against me and we stood so for some time. I felt the old longing, but it was tainted somehow—distracted. Everything was upset.

"How long will you be here, my love?"

"Spintharus was just asking the same thing. I don't know."

"A few days?"

"Perhaps."

"Have you been working hard?"

"Exceedingly." We had begun to talk more openly of my earning manumission. Suddenly, that hope seemed doubtful.

"Has he said anything?"

"He offered me some advice from Quintus Tullius—'Give your ship over to the winds, but never your soul to a woman.'"

She laughed again, stepped back and wiped her other eye. "That sounds like Quintus."

"Have you heard anything of him? Of any of our master's relatives?"

She shrugged. "Young Marcus—"

"In Greece, yes. What of Quintus's son? We last saw them together. Have they split up?"

"You see, Leonidas, you know more than I or anyone else on this estate, probably."

I nodded and looked back toward the temple on the coast, but could not now spot it. Clementia led me to a low bench beside the house, between two rose bushes grey with the winter. We sat.

"You seem worried, my love."

"I don't think I had realized how much danger we were in until now, here with you."

"How so?"

"Marcus Tullius is in danger of his life. Antonius has

proscribed him, him and all his family and associates."

"It was those speeches, wasn't it?"

"He says there's more to it than that."

"You are a strong man, Leonidas. Our master is a strong man. Marcus Antonius is not. You accuse a weak man with a strong wife of incest and see what happens."

I laughed despite myself. "Marcus Tullius has always prided himself on being the most unpopular man in Rome."

"Politics," she said. "Why do you think I slip out of the kitchen when he lies down to dinner?"

I laughed.

"So—he no longer has young Caesar's protection? Caesar's friendship?"

I shook my head. Tears started to Clementia's eyes again.

"What will become of us?"

"I don't know," I said, and at that moment spied a man on horseback, far below the villa on a bend in the road to Formiae, riding like Apollo in his chariot. I stood and squinted down to catch a glimpse—dark clothing, not military—before he disappeared from sight, headed our way. I kissed Clementia and made for the front door.

*

29

I KNEW THE MESSENGER—PHILOLOGUS, A YOUNG GREEK freedman of Quintus's household. I met him at the door of the house as he reined his lathered horse in hard and rolled laterally from its back. He thumped to the road and whoofed all the air from his lungs. It was some time before he could rise and yet longer until he could catch enough breath to speak, and by then our master had sent Gesataia, a Gaulish serving girl, to ask what the commotion was.

I could see from Philologus's face that something was amiss.

We brought him inside. Somehow, the whole household knew already that someone from Quintus's household was come and had crowded into the entryway. They craned around doorposts and stood tip-toe behind the others to see. I saw Clementia's blonde twist of hair bobbing near the back, out in the garden colonnade. I thought for a moment that it may be better if she did not hear what news we were about to receive from Quintus. How was I to know that, in time, we would see worse than we were to hear?

Gnaeus stopped us in the doorway to the dining room and looked Philologus over. He gestured for him to remove his riding cloak, which he handed to me, then turned him this way and that, ran his hands over him, through his sleeves, and under the skirt of his tunic. Philologus was too exhausted, it seemed, to object. At last, Gnaeus nodded to me and stepped aside. Philologus entered and presented himself to my master.

As I followed, Gnaeus murmured, "I did not like the look of him."

I nodded to him and entered the dining room.

I could tell that Marcus Tullius had read Philologus's face much the way I had. His own face bore a drained, haggard look, the look he had when he rose aboard ship that morning, but mingled with something else. When he spoke, I knew from his voice—so artfully concealed, it would have fooled the Senate or an assembly, but not a household slave—from a tiny tremor, a handful of halting words, that his seasick look was now mingled with fear.

"And what news do you bring from my brother, friend Philologus? Why does he not write?"

"Senator, I beg your pardon——"

Fear gave way to the need for confirmation, to know: "Be direct. Out with it."

"Quintus Tullius Cicero is dead. Your brother is dead."

"Merely dead, or murdered?"

"The latter, sir."

Gasps, and a scream from one of the women of the kitchen. Only then did he allow some show. His face fell yet further. What would have been a histrionic moan from any other came out as a long, resigned sigh. Tiro put his hand to his eyes and stepped away. Germanicus said nothing, but reached from his couch to place a hand on my master's shoulder. I looked back at Gnaeus. His face had tightened, his jaw set, and his eyes burned. Only later did I understand that, beneath the anger was also sorrow. He stood on the verge of tears.

For my part, I listened as if to a stage play. Only as we continued to talk did I grasp the things we talked about. My master's brother murdered—this had happened. Marcus Antoniushad caught up not with my master, but with his family first. My stomach knotted.

"I'm afraid there is more," Philologus said. "His son as well, killed with him."

The cries of the household now bore a note of panic. My master roused himself and said, with a voice that was not a shout but yet filled the house, "Enough. We will mourn. Go about your duties and we will mourn."

He raised a hand to Philologus and held it there until the household had dispersed. At last, the house stood unnaturally quiet, as if it had become a great ear for the scattered but listening servants.Remaining behind in the dining room were my master, his guest Germanicus, Tiro, Spintharus, Gnaeus, the sea captain, Philologus, and myself.

My master first lowered his hand, and then lowered his head. "Go on."

"You will recall that, when last our households were together, your brother and nephew decided to return home."

"Yes." That was a hard day—the old brothers and friends, side by side in their sedan chairs on the shoulder of the Appian Way, Quintus on the edge of cracking, Marcus torn by indecision, finally taking leave of each other.

"We went back to the villa in Tusculum, where Quintus Tullius intended to provision himself separately for an escape to Greece and the forces of Junius Brutus. He intended to spent two days there, no more, but stayed three. Near dusk on the third day a squadron of auxiliary cavalry led by two centurions from one of Marcus Antonius's legions arrived. We don't know how they tracked us down so quickly, unless they had been making regular patrols to Quintus's and—his known residences."

"Marcus Antonius is hardly so thorough," my master said, and rested his chin in his palm. I looked at Philologus. Something about the way he had hesitated, as though about to include my master in the theory of Antonius's stalking, struck me as odd. One learns a lot working for an orator. I was surprised my master had missed it. Perhaps he had not.

Philologus, for his part, missed the barb aimed at Antonius. "Sir?"

"Go on."

"Your nephew, young Quintus, immediately hid your brother in a secret compartment under the oil and wine storeroom. You know the place."

"Yes."

"The centurions arrived at the head of their force and tore the house apart. They broke up the furniture, dug through the garden, broke open barrels and chests, and piled up what was too valuable to smash in the entryway to take back with them. The auxiliaries raped some of the slave girls, too, and desecrated the images of your fathers in the entryway."

My master sat up and clumsily dashed a clenched fist against his eyes. He trembled with rage. "What next?"

"Failing to find your brother, they took young Quintus to the garden, tied him between two of the columns, and beat him. First with fists, then with odds and ends from among the broken furniture, and finally with a whip—the tails. He never cried out, but fainted dead away twice. Both times they revived him by pouring entire pots of water over his face until he choked and turned blue, and then resumed the beating. He would not give up your brother. Finally, though young Quintus never cried or screamed, the noise of what was going on couldn't be missed, and your brother broke his way out of the trap door in the store room, and presented himself to the soldiers. He begged them, as fellow Romans and fellow soldiers—he called on the memory of Julius Caesar, whom they had both served in Gaul—to release his son, who had borne their abuse like a true Roman should, and to take him instead."

"Glorious courage," Germanicus said.

"But not, apparently, honored by Antonius," my master said.

"No," Philologus said.

Marcus Tullius heaved another sigh and sat up straight on his dining couch to receive the end of the story. By his example, even the old Censor struggled up from his couch to sit upright. My master reminded me, for a moment, of the old Senators who met the conquering Gauls with fierce dignity, gravity, and heart, hundreds of years ago when Rome was sacked. It only occurred to me later that the Gauls, after some initial admiration, killed the Senators.

"What then?"

"The soldiers talked amongst themselves and finally agreed to release young Quintus. 'We have a doctor with us,' they said.

'We'll patch him up and escort him to Tusculum, where he can stay with a doctor of your choosing. Then he can take ship for Greece or wherever. You come with us to Marcus Antonius.' They split up, took young Quintus down, and carried him out of the house. Quintus Tullius the other half escorted, after first allowing him to put on a clean toga with the badge of his rank on it. Once on the road, with the two parties still within sight of each other, the centurions gave a signal they had agreed on in the house and threw father and son to the road and cut off their heads."

Somewhere back in the house, I heard a woman sob. Germanicus sat ashen, and Tiro stood so behind him. My master sat silent. Finally, he nodded. "They need worry about Marcus Antonius no more," he said.

When Gnaeus spoke from the doorway, I jumped. "How did you learn all this?"

Philologus looked at him. "What?"

"How did you learn all this? Given that you escaped."

"Ah—" Philologus looked from Gnaeus to my master and back. "I hid, like Quintus Tullius. I heard everything."

Gnaeus grunted and said no more.

"What of their burial?" my master said.

"I don't know," Philologus said. "The cavalry left their

bodies in the road. The heads they took to Marcus Antonius."

"I do not need to know to what foul use Antonius will put them. Or his whore, that Fulvia. Their depravities know no end." He looked at us one by one, and rose. "Thank you, Philologus. You have always served our families well. I am sorry the last duty you paid to my brother was this one. Spintharus, see that Philologus gets food and rest."

Spintharus ushered Philologus from the dining room. Gnaeus stepped aside to make way, and as they passed, he shot me a look. Philologus may have carried no weapon, but Gnaeus suspected him nonetheless.

Marcus Tullius turned to Germanicus, who still sat, stunned, on his couch. "I'm sorry, my friend, that your visit should end this way, but I think it best for your own sake that you go. Rome owes its faithful statesmen at least one natural death."

"Tullius," Germanicus said. "You must flee. If they found your brother—"

"Yes, yes."

Germanicus stared at him. "Have you no fear?"

"Of course. But you as well as I know that a Roman will not be unmanned by fear."

"Yes."

"How far Rome has fallen," my master said, "when her statesmen—no, they are all generals now, generals only. How far has she fallen when the claims of duty and love have been replaced with brute fear. Give Caesar his laws or die. Kiss Antonius's ass or die. Cato prayed we should never see another Sulla. The merciful gods have not allowed him to live to see a succession of them. A team of Sullas, even! Force isn't even their first resort—Catilina, that conspirator I uncovered and foiled, at least tried to use sneakery and force, instead of bullying and insinuating fear and betrayal into the lives of every decent citizen. But I suppose force only works on brave men—for everyone else, the fear of force will suffice. No, I will not be ruled by fear. No Roman was ever ruled by any man, much less a mere emotion."

We stood in silence for a time. I had listened to many of my master's speeches—enough so that I could take notes by hand while thinking of entirely different subjects—but never had I heard him speak so briefly with so much feeling.

Before I could stop myself, I said: "You will make a fine speaker someday, sir."

They laughed, and my master sat again. He took one more drink of wine and smiled. "Thank you for coming today, Germanicus. Your friendship has meant a great deal. Please remember me to your family and to the gods."

Germanicus, resigned, rose and walked to the door. "And my thanks to you, Marcus Tullius Cicero, for all your service."

My master waved him off. Germanicus, before he turned to leave my master's villa for the last time, said, "What will you do?"

"Stay."

"And if they catch you?"

My master sat up again like those Senators of ancient days and said, "Die, serving the country I so often saved."

*

HE DISMISSED TIRO AND THE CAPTAIN OF THE SHIP and had us stoke the fires for a bath. While he bathed and received a shave—only a shave, unfortunately, since we did not have a barber—he had the slaves fully unpack the things we had unloaded from the ship that morning. Once bathed, shaved, and dressed, he halted along the garden colonnade and shut himself in his library. Gnaeus stood watch outside.

As we worked, I caught occasional sight of Clementia. She and her help were busy preparing the dining room for the evening meal—set for my master and his one or two assistants.

39

Her eyes were swollen and bloodshot. Even so long after Philologus's arrival she sniffled. Once when we passed each other in the entry hall I caught her gently by the elbow.

She turned her head but did not go. "I'm busy, Leonidas."

"Everything will be all right."

She shook her head and rubbed her nose with the back of a hand. "You know as well as I—"

"Everything will be all right."

"What of us now?"

I bit my lip and lowered my head. Our master would be all right—that much we knew. But for us there was more than his life at risk.

Once finished, I went to find him. Gnaeus greeted me grimly at the door to the library and let me in.

Marcus Tullius stood reading a scroll by the window. It was by now mid-afternoon, and the light was better there. I could see the slaves had unloaded and set up his tall writing table near the window, and arranged his ink and writing instruments for immediate use. On the sill beside him, at the height of his failing hip, lay an open wax tablet, stylus, and a few slips of papyrus. The papyrus was deeply creased, and I made out the small, crabbed, but evenly-spaced writing of Tullia. I halted just inside the threshold. As I decided to leave, my master looked up.

"Please come in, Leonidas. No need to hesitate."

"I'm sorry to interrupt, sir. I just came to say we have finished the unpacking."

"Thank you, Leonidas. And no need for an apology—you're not interrupting. I know this work well."

I looked at Tullia's letters in the sunlight on the sill. "Sir?"

He lifted the scroll. "*Medea.*"

The tragedy, by a Greek—Euripides. I was not much for drama. "Ah. Very good, sir."

"It was a favorite of my daughter's," he said. "She gave me this copy some years ago."

I did not know what to say, and so kept silent. After a time, my master chuckled fondly.

"Such a thing for a girl to enjoy—a wild woman butchering her own flesh and blood, borne away in a dragon-drawn chariot. Spared any penalty. The whole world, every duty we owe each other upended. Everything upset. So unlike my dear Tullia."

"I'm sorry, sir."

He lowered and rolled the scroll.

"I have some books in cases you unloaded this morning. Please bring me a case that will fit this. The one containing the Elder Cato's speeches should do."

41

"And the speeches?"

He nodded to the racks lining one wall of the room. Threescore books or more, a rich stock for a country villa, slotted neatly in their racks. Their identifying tags, suspended from the outer handle, turned slowly with the motes in the sunlight. "We can leave that volume here."

I went to his office but the books were not there. The other slaves had not apparently given much attention to what our master would want. I found them on the small table beside his bed and dug out the case containing the *Orations* of Cato the Elder. I ran a hand over the scroll and thought of the great man's great-grandson, whose bloody memory Clementia and I had invoked. An entire family of great men, defending the Republic, honored for service stretching back past our tawdry recent troubles to the days of Scipio Africanus and Hannibal. The Republic had a long memory. Individuals came and went—inevitably, unavoidably so, as my master's philosophy reminded us—but the Republic, like its families, could last forever. And a good name could keep a man alive for centuries after his body had burnt to ash and all that remained of him was a beeswax mask in the entry hall.

My master, even now past his sixtieth year, was a newcomer. He did not come from a line like Cato's—or, for that matter,

Caesar's—but was a New Man, the first of his line to attain senatorial rank. Now he seemed determined to remain in Italy and die. The ash and the mask could come sooner than any of us may have thought.

I wondered for a moment what future generations would make of him. Would they still copy his speeches? Would senators carry them around, reading in their sedan chairs as my master now did Cato the Elder? Would a renewed Republic keep his memory alive, as my master kept the memory of his fathers alive every morning at the household altar? A family could last forever—young Marcus was gone, and could yet survive. He had at last grown into a good, strong man, a keen soldier, and would make a fine senator someday. But to think of my master murdered, proscribed by a tyrant after a lifetime of service—I could not bear it.

I came to myself when a sob escaped me. I looked about to be sure I was alone, then wiped my eyes and closed up the book case. I went back to the library.

Marcus Tullius turned back to me from the window when I entered and immediately began to speak, but stopped short.

"Leonidas—you've—what has happened?"

My eyes had betrayed me, as Clementia's swollen eyes had her. "Nothing I cannot bear, sir."

He set down the papyrus leaf he had been reading—one of the letters—and came closer. He took the case from me and removed Cato's speeches from it. He looked at the scroll and then at me.

"It is unlike you to weep at the Old Roman, and unlike him to cause tears. What is the matter?"

"Nothing, sir."

"Oh, come off it. Tears are nothing to be ashamed of in this house on this day. Is it my brother? I mourn him myself. He would not want—"

"No, master. It is you."

In all his pride, he had never expected that. And that was why we loved him.

"Me?"

"Yes, sir. I—"

"You fear I will be killed before I can free you? A mere formality, Leonidas. You have more than earned it. I—"

"No, sir," and, when I realized what he was saying, "I mean, yes, sir. I desire that more than anything. I want my freedom. You yourself have said that a slave has no life. I want life, and I want to buy Clementia's freedom, and I want a family of my own. I desire all these things but—I amaze myself—I would give them up to preserve your life, sir." He stepped back and stared. I continued. "You will die, sir."

"Even a young man should not count on living through the day, Leonidas."

"We all die, I know it, but you deserve better, sir. Marcus Tullius Cicero has given his life to the Republic. He foiled Catilina and outlasted Clodius and lived to see Julius Caesar struck down. He cannot die now, at the hands of Caesar's whoreson lackey. Dying at the hands of Marcus Antonius is unworthy of you, and Marcus Antonius is unworthy of the satisfaction."

My master surprised me then—he laughed, a deep, hearty laugh such as we had not heard from him in a year or more.

"My man Leonidas. An excellent construction—we will make an orator of you yet."

"I'm serious, sir."

He waved a hand. "I know, and I am deeply touched. I thank you. One moment—"

He stepped back to the window, took up a blank leaf of papyrus, and limped to his writing table. From the same pot which had provided him ink to compose his speeches and pamphlets against Antonius, he scribbled a letter of manumission for me—and Clementia.

"This is an informal notice. For full citizenship, which I

desire for you, we will have to have the approval of the magistrates, but this is a bad time to be conducting business in Rome. I hope this will suffice for now." He blotted the papyrus, blew on it, and handed it to me. "Keep the money you would have used to redeem her. Buy a farm, far from the city. Have twenty sons and name them all for me."

I tried to speak and nothing came. He laughed again. "Yes, the girl may have something to say about that. But thank you again, Leonidas. You are a free man. You can go, if you wish."

I looked at the papyrus and tried to keep my thumbs out of the ink. It was all there, in Marcus Tullius's fine script so that everyone could read it. I looked at him, now clean and shaven but still a heavy, grey, buckling version of the man who had bought me years before. I gripped the papyrus and made a decision.

"If you stay, I stay," I said.

For a moment he seemed to look down on me from Olympian height, and then he paid me the greatest compliment of my life: "You are more an Old Roman than many Romans today." And then, a moment later, "Certainly more so than the murderers who will capture me."

My chest swelled. "We will not let that happen, Marcus Tullius."

He lowered his head and sat—slowly—on the windowsill. He laid a hand on Tullia's letters and fingered them absently. "Do not risk yourself or your future for me, Leonidas."

"I know how to use a sword."

"Bosh. Any brute can use a sword. That foul army catamite Antonius can use a sword, as we all know. And by Hercules, we know the sword has been used on him, too." He paused and I laughed. Many today do not appreciate his deft touch for comedy—abuse, specifically. He went on. "No, life is not merely drawing breath. I am a tired old man. Grouchy, dyspeptic more often than not. My limbs ache. My hip bothers me. Don't look surprised—I know you know. I have troubled dreams. I dream—of Tullia. And of my father sometimes. I lived a long and good life for my country, and even when I stop drawing breath I will have some kind of life because of it."

I looked at him. "Must we protect you from yourself?"

"No," he said. "I will not kill myself. That is contrary to Nature."

"But Marcus Porcius Cato—"

"Of the dead, nothing but good, Leonidas. Surely you know me better than that. But I will not flee. We do not know what Fate has in store for us. Best to embrace our duties and endure. And that is what I mean—you are a free man, and owe me nothing more. Get out while you can. Risk nothing on account of a tired old Senator."

I thought a moment and looked again at the manumission. The ink had dried. I had one smear on my thumb.

"If I may, Marcus Tullius, I would like to go find Clementia."

He made a sweeping oratorical gesture toward the door. "Please. And do not ask permission of me again."

I stood and opened the door. Gnaeus peeked in and stepped back. I turned. Marcus Tullius had hoisted himself to his feet and unspooled *Medea* again.

"Senator?" I said.

He looked up.

"You were wrong about one thing. I do owe you. When I was a slave I had no life, and now as a free man you urge me to defend my life. It seems to me that even free men owe service to the thing that gives them life. For you, that is the Republic. For me, that is you."

He nodded and was quiet for a long time. When he spoke, I recognized the tone beneath his words—gratitude.

"Your logic is sound. I will have to find a way to refute you. Marcus Tullius Cicero is never wrong."

I left him—a free man's privilege—to find and tell

Clementia the good news. Only later, reflecting on my conversation with him, did I realize that he had spoken of his murder like a foregone conclusion.

*

GNAEUS HAD OVERHEARD, AND WAS THE FIRST TO congratulate me. He clapped me on the back and sent me looking for Clementia with some soldierly advice on what to do with her to celebrate. I glanced into the bedrooms I passed along the garden colonnade and then crossed to the servant's entrance to the kitchen. When I entered the dark and smoky room, I tripped and nearly brained myself on the floor. I caught myself and looked back. Philologus, the late Quintus's freedman, sat sprawled in the dark beside the doorway gnawing the remainder of a barley loaf. I had tripped over his foot. He stared at me.

"Leonidas!" he said when he recovered himself. "I'm sorry."

I brushed myself off and rubbed my aching palms against my thighs. I could not be angry at him. Nothing—even my master's resignation—could ruin my spirits. How quickly and how often a man's mind can be upended in the space of an hour.

"No harm done, Philologus," I said. "Say, have you seen Clementia?"

"Clementia?"

"She runs the kitchen."

"Oh, the buxom German? What do you want with her?"

"Marriage," I said.

"So to speak, eh?"

"No, literally. Marcus Tullius has just given me my freedom, and hers as well. We intend to marry and start a family."

"Ah, well congratulations. Do enjoy her for me."

I could not rise above mere annoyance at even these insults. "As if you would know what to do, Greekling. Never mind—I'll find her myself."

One of the slave girls told me Clementia had gone outside on some errand. I thanked her and left through the dining room. I looked back at Philologus as I left. He seemed unbothered by anything—not my barbs, not the death of his former master or the grave possibility of the death of mine—and content to mop up some oil from a bowl with the rind of his loaf.

I found Clementia in the herb garden at the back of the house. A fine late afternoon breeze had blown in off the sea, and far off we could hear sea birds. She worked alone—she had sent her usual help, an elderly Greek woman named Acte and the Gaulish girl called Gesataia, down to Formiae to visit the market before the day grew too long. I held up the papyrus and read it to her. She nearly bowled me over in an embrace. In her excitement, it was some time before she reverted to Latin from her native tongue.

"You have your savings, Leonidas! We should leave! Gather our things and leave. But of course thank our master first, before——" She remembered Marcus Tullius's situation and halted. Her eyes widened. "Leonidas, we must leave. Surely you have thought of this. What will happen when they catch him? Happen to us?"

I took a moment too long to answer and she stepped back and regarded me coldly.

"Clementia, we owe him our lives."

"Not like this. No."

"He was ever good to us and now we have our freedom. The least we should do——"

"Is leave. You heard what Philologus saw in Quintus's house. They were not torturing a slave for a confession—they tortured a free man. He said they raped the women."

"That won't happen."

"You have heard Quintus talk about what happened to the

women after a battle. After a city falls. Antonius's men are not waiting for cities. They are practicing on houses."

"I won't let that happen."

"What will you do about it?"

"Fight."

Clementia moaned. "How?"

"Gnaeus Mucius, Marcus Tullius's bodyguard, is a retired centurion. He has decades of experience in the legions."

"One man."

"We can barricade the house, arm the litter bearers and baggage men. They are mostly young and all strong."

Clementia's moan climbed toward a wail. "Slaves, Leonidas, like yourself until half an hour ago."

"Like us, Clementia." She looked at me, waiting. "We owe Marcus Tullius so much. Can we not give back to him now? When all have deserted him?" She nodded and stepped into my arms. "He has lost everything he ever held dear."

"What? The Republic?"

"Perhaps. But what about his brother? His nephew? Tullia?"

Clementia shut her eyes and lowered her head. "Yes, of course."

Tullia had been our master's only daughter, his favorite child. Long before I came into the household she was a dear dark-eyed girl, mischievous, intelligent, and strong-willed. Her father recognized himself in her and doted—but did not spoil her. She grew into a quick-witted and resourceful woman. Again, her father saw himself in her. His fondness for her strained his Old Roman dignity—he was often seen to smile at her in public. His enemies accused him of incest, the only insult I ever saw him laugh off as too ridiculous to countenance. She married three times—the first two times happily, all three times with her father's reluctance. They maintained a steady and affectionate correspondence wherever either of them went. The letters continued even after his divorce from her and young Marcus's mother, our old mistress Terentia, and his remarriage to a young woman I will not name. I never knew Tullia as the clever roundfaced toddler he and the older slaves so often and so fondly recalled, but she was always kind to me, and to Clementia.

Then, a little over a year before Julius Caesar's death, she bore a stillborn child. She seemed to recover but suddenly hemorrhaged and died. My master, in the eyes of his enemies and even many friends, unmanned himself with grief. His new wife was no comfort—if anything, she was glad to be rid of a rival for the old man's affection. He divorced her and left the city. He visited his friends in Italy and abroad and plundered their libraries of philosophy for comfort, but found little. Those were hard times, with much travel. He put on weight and the aches and pains of age—the hand, the hip, a variety of other complaints—worsened. When at last he had recovered somewhat, and written and published his *Self-Consolation*, he returned to public life, just in time for the murder of Caesar and the crisis now coming to fulfilment.

All that remained to him of his life before was his son, abroad and in danger, this villa, a figurine and some letters. All else had burnt to ash.

"I feel like I have lost everything with him," I said.

"I too, my love," she said. "Do you not feel it, too? Like we've gained and lost everything in this one talk? When you read me his writing I saw us leaving for the mountains and getting us some land. I saw you turning the earth and planting for me and our children, and then our strong sons doing the same, and their sons coming to us in our old age. I saw and enjoyed our freedom together in the space of a moment. How can you give this up, Leonidas?"

I did not answer for some time. At last, I said, "I don't think I am."

"Does it not hurt you to think that none of that will come to pass?"

"Yes. Terribly."

"Then take me and leave this place. Save us."

I let her go and buried my head in my hands. When at last I looked up, I saw the distant shore and heard not seabirds, but crows. As if called, one appeared from the tree tops and alighted on a post at the end of the garden. I shuddered.

"Did you hear, Clementia, about the omen?"

"What omen? There are many."

"The crows this morning."

"That flew on our master's ship? Yes. Is the meaning not plain to you?"

I regarded the crow, and he me. "No."

Clementia wiped tears from her eyes. "Our master will die, Leonidas. Why should we die with him?"

"We owe him."

"Do you not owe me?"

"Yes. But not without owing him first."

Her lip trembled like a child's and she wept, her vision of freedom replaced with one of death. "Is there no other way?"

I raised my empty palms, a gesture learned from my master. I had nothing—no other plan, no means of comfort. I pulled her to me again, and as I did so I saw the crow, as if he had completed a task, bound away and take flight. I cursed him and all his kind.

"I'm sorry, Clementia. This is not the reunion either of us wanted."

"You are here. That is all I wanted."

"I won't let anything happen to you."

"I donot care. I donot want anything to happen to you."

I thought of my conversation with Marcus Tullius in the library. I felt chains of duties, offices gravely fulfilled, stretching from himself through me to Clementia. Without those duties, nothing. And yet they had never felt so much like chains.

We went inside and the women of the kitchen, who had heard the news, swarmed Clementia to congratulate her. I went in search of my master. Freedom already felt like a burden.

*

I DID NOT HAVE TO LOOK FAR. I SAW GNAEUS STANDING guard outside his bedroom door and approached. He grinned at me.

"Well?"

"Well what?"

He looked confused, and then he marked my face, tear-streaked again. "What happened?"

56

"I told her, and told her as well that I meant to stay with Marcus Tullius until the end."

"Oh. Oh, Leonidas."

"What am I to do?"

"Not that."

"What would you have done?"

"Don't ask me. The only women I've ever had were whores. Limits the commitment."

I glared at him.

"All right—I still don't know, but I admire your honesty toward her and toward the Senator."

"I'm only doing what he would have done."

"Don't be so sure. But you are doing your duty by him."

"That's why I am here. I'd like to talk to him again."

Gnaeus shook his head. "Sleeping."

"A nap?"

"He's an old man, Leonidas. He thought well enough of you to say so himself."

"Yes," I said. At least I had Gnaeus to talk to. "I want to arm the household, barricade the doors and windows. He may mean to stay, but that does not mean he has to die undefended, friendless. Surely we owe him that much."

"I'm hired help."

"You know what I mean, and you're no mercenary."

Gnaeus looked hard at me. "You know what you and the Senator have in common? I'm serious. You are both new men who care more about what it means to be an Old Roman than the really old Romans do."

He had lost me. "What? What does that have to do with—"

He held up a hand. "Look at Antonius. Julius Caesar. Young Caesar, in all likelihood, though I wouldn't give up on the boy yet. Look at those old families and the circles in which they move. They have been the heart of Rome since the beginning but what do they care for it? It's a bauble, to be fought over by every power-mad and debauched man who can hire a handful of gladiators for the mob. By Dis, look at me. You know the story of Lucius Mucius Scaevola?"

"The Left-Handed, yes." The family was still prominent—my master's tutor had been a direct descendent of this ancient hero.

"Sent to assassinate the Etruscan king. Captured by the enemy. Burned his own damn hand off rather than renege on an oath and dishonor his country. 'Romans fight bravely and, when thing go against us, we suffer bravely.' What has become of the clan of Mucius? Look at Gnaeus Mucius. Hireling soldier. A career bachelor, with ten women in every camp town. No exaggeration, mind you. No wife. Never even made it to a farm.

No Old Roman ever took pay to fight. No Old Roman would avoid marriage and risk the extinction of his line. No Old Roman would settle for anything but his farm and hearth, the honor of his fathers and the hearth-goddess."

"You speak too much ill of yourself, Gnaeus."

"I could go on. But no—what you and the Senator, the son of a merchant, have in common is more respect for the past, for the traditions that made the Republic possible, than the people enjoying its fruits. And one will have to give place to the other, sooner or later."

I thought a long time. At last, I said, "I thought you weren't much for speeches."

"Well, I say that and then go and embarrass myself like that."

"I don't know about any of that, but I thank you, and I think we owe it to men like Marcus Tullius to defend them. As long as there are the two kinds you describe, the kind like him will need it."

"I don't disagree."

"Then will you help us? Even if the cash dries up?"

"After all that? I had better help, especially if the cash dries up."

I grinned—happy to be doing duty as a Roman so soon

after being a slave—and nodded to the door. "Shall we tell him?"

Gnaeus hesitated. "What about the others?"

"What others? The household?"

"You haven't heard of the slaves who dragged their masters in for the reward—or outright helped to kill them—during Sulla's proscriptions?"

"Yes, of course. But no one here would do that."

"I would find out. If anything, they're likely to run off, slaves being slaves. Meaning no offense to an upstanding freedman, of course."

I thought on it. Gnaeus was right. I had no guarantee that the others in the household would feel so dutifully as the two of us did. Even Clementia, who loved me, remained only for that reason.

I sought out Spintharus. He agreed enthusiastically with the plan to defend our master. He joined me and together we caught every member of the household, whether at chores or resting between tasks, and gauged their loyalty to Marcus Tullius. Every one, whether enthusiastically or strictly out of piety for the bonds of duty, volunteered to stay and defend him. The only people we did not speak to were Acte and Gesataia, the women still absent at the market, and Philologus, whom one slave girl said she had seen making for the back of the house, presumably to lie down in one of the guest rooms. We did not bother about him, as he was not technically a member of the household.

Our canvass accomplished, Spintharus and I reported back to Gnaeus, who seemed heartened at the news. I think we thought it might work then, in that brief happy hour of the afternoon. Gnaeus knocked once on Marcus Tullius's door and we entered.

We found my master lying diagonally across his bed, on his right side. He had opened the window, and the far sound of the sea came in. He had kept his toga on but pulled it up over his head in the old-fashioned way to cover it while he slept. All that was visible of him was his hands, the right one curled stiffly under his bulk. He must have been resting peacefully, because while I had expected him to sit up and—dyspeptic—ask why we had roused him from his late-afternoon nap, he lay still. Only the toga about his midsection, in its rising and fall, gave any indication that he still lived.

Gnaeus cleared his throat and the form on the bed moved heavily. My master grunted.

"Senator, I apologize for disturbing you, but a few of us wish to speak with you."

My master raised himself stiffly on his right elbow and pulled the toga away from his head. He gave us one bleary eyed look and sat up.

"Gnaeus Mucius," he said. "Spintharus. Leonidas. What has happened? What's the trouble?"

"Nothing, sir," I said.

"Nothing new, that is," Gnaeus said.

Marcus Tullius eyed us and worked absently with his stiffened right hand, the middle finger in particular. He raised himself and struck one of his old oratorical poses, as if ready to speak, and regarded us in silence. It occurred to me only years afterward that, in that moment, he probably thought that we had come to kill him. He was prepared already.

"We have spoken to the whole household, sir," Spintharus said, "and we mean to arm ourselves and defend you."

He regarded us yet a moment more, weighed our intent, then relaxed from his pose, rubbed his hip, and smiled. "No," he said.

We looked at each other. "Sir?" Spintharus said.

He sat on the bed. "No."

I stepped forward. "We have discussed it thoroughly. Barricades on the doors and windows. We have ample food and a store of knives in the kitchen and some old army swords.

Gnaeus himself, as you know, is well armed, and will lead us."

"This was your idea."

"Yes, master. Marcus Tullius."

"We cannot hold out indefinitely," Gnaeus said, "but we could perhaps outlast a detachment from Antonius's camp in the north. By then a deal could be struck. Young Caesar may change his mind yet again."

My old master—I was having trouble thinking of him as anything else, trouble which persists to this day, as you will have noticed—shook his head and said again, "No."

We stood in silence. We would have denied it if stated so baldly, but we had expected thanks, fawning over our initiative, the praise of a great man. We were in that moment no better than Marcus Antonius's hangers on, or Julius Caesar's lackeys before them.

"But, sir," I said.

Marcus Tullius raised his hand. "What will happen to you, truly, even if you resist a detachment—one such as you describe, Gnaeus Mucius? What will happen to the people of this household when the doors are broken in and all of you who still have swords in your hands lie spattered in blood on the floor?"

"We have considered the consequences," I said, but I saw

from Spintharus's expression that he, at least, had not.

"I will tell you. The women, probably ravished—from the girls on up to old Acte the gardener, one and all—will be whipped and resold if they are not murdered once the soldiers are done with them. Your men will be crucified. You know that. Spartacus's men, rotting on crosses, did not line that road down the hill so long ago that you don't know what the fate of a fighting slave is. I say again, no. Go. All of you. I am the master of this household and it is my duty to keep you all safe. Leave me while you can. That is all I will say of it."

With that, he turned from us and stretched out again, and hid his face from us beneath his toga. We left him there.

"What now?" Spintharus said.

"I don't know," I said.

"Arm yourselves anyway," Gnaeus us. "Before what he said gets out." He gave Spintharus a look, and Spintharus looked away.

"We can't leave him," I said.

"He won't have it," Spintharus said.

"I have to think," Gnaeus said. He rubbed his eyes furiously with the heels of his palms. I looked around to be sure we were alone, and saw Clementia watching us from the kitchen door across the garden. I watched her. She knew. Somehow, she knew. She turned and went back into the kitchen.

"Wait here," I said.

I pushed through the naked, twiggy garden and into the kitchen. She stood with her back to one of the tables where they prepared the meals. Three other women were at work on supper. They looked up and smiled when they recognized me, then seemed to remember that we had other considerations than our manumission, lowered their eyes, and went back to work. I nodded to the dining room door and Clementia walked through it. I followed.

She reached the dining room window, the one open to the sea, and turned on me.

"He wants us to leave. I can tell."

"Clementia—"

"Leonidas, he wants us to go. Wants us to. I know you love that old man—we all do—but let him die alone as he wishes. Let us leave."

I shook my head. I wanted to do everything and nothing. Was this what warring against Fate felt like?

"We can't leave him."

"He wants us to. So that we do not suffer like Quintus's people."

I looked at her. She searched my face. I looked out the

window. The westering sun was in its descent, but still an hour or so from dusk. The sky had begun to turn colors, a gold drawing red and purple up from the horizon.

"I do not want you to suffer, or anyone," I said. "I want to take in this sunset with you again and again from some land of our own. I want to make love to you on evenings like this." I gestured out the window and down the hill. "Like we used to in the lane."

She leaned toward me and said, in a voice that was less a whisper than a hiss, "Then take us from here now."

Before I could reply, I heard frantic noise outside. I leaned out the window and squinted against the slanting sun. Up the hill staggered two crouched forms, one struggling as if under a great weight, the other hovering about the first, ducking back and forth, alternately urging the first on and uttering panicked whimpers that I could not understand. They crested the hill and made for the servants' entrance to the kitchen, and I knew them—old Acte and Gesataia, the Gaulish girl, returned from Formiae. And they had come up not by the main road from the highway into town, but by the hidden lane Clementia and I had just spoken of. Once on level ground, the little Gaul broke for the house, babbling in that peculiar tongue of the Celts, and left the old woman hobbling alone.

66

Clementia and I met Gesataia at the door. Her hair was disheveled and her face blanched with fear and streaked with sweat. Her eyes were wide. I had only heard this appearance described—in Quintus's war stories from Gaul. Panic, flight, defeat and retreat. She saw us and her chatter pitched yet higher. She fell to her knees before Clementia and clutched at her dress, beseeching.

"What—what is it? What is it, Gesataia?" Clementia said, and then lapsed into her own tongue. The fear was spreading.

I stood and watched. At last, Acte, heaving with each breath, came up and slung a bundle of vegetables and fresh fish to the ground before us. She straightened her back as much as she could manage, looked me in the eye, and said: "Soldiers. In town. The freedman has given us up to Marcus Antonius's soldiers."

*

WE PIECED IT TOGETHER QUICKLY. PHILOLOGUS HAD come to tell us about Quintus's fate, yes, but also as a spy. He knew Marcus Tullius's estates from Quintus's visits and could lead Antonius's men to my master. He had sold my master out, and probably had Quintus as well.

Acte and Gesataia had seen him in town approaching some armed soldiers outside a cobbler's shop, and after asking a few careful questions of bystanders, learned that their leaders were Herennius, a centurion of one of Antonius's legions, and Gaius Popillius Laenas, a military tribune from the same. Acte understood the danger to be much more immediate than we had reckoned. Gesataia was for bolting back the villa to raise the alarm. Acte, a Greek, and therefore more cunning, decided to browse unhurriedly for what they came to buy and leave town at a regular pace—and to be seen doing so. Once out of sight among the tombs along the Appian Way, they ducked into the shaded lane Clementia and I had shared so often and hastened back. Gesataia, already unnerved to move so deliberately under the enemy's eyes, grew more panicked with every agonizing step the old woman took. But at last they had returned. How much time we had none could know.

I turned and ran through the house to Gnaeus, still watching at my master's door.

"Antonius's men are in Formiae," I said. "Philologus, the freedman from Quintus's household, has tipped them off."

Gnaeus's face hardened. "Weapons?"

"This way."

I led him to the back of the house. We grabbed and

gathered into a retinue every male slave and member of the household we passed. When we reached the storeroom, we had a dozen men—myself and Gnaeus, wide-eyed Spintharus, the seven other litter bearers, and two of Acte's grandsons, unbearded youths just old enough to be called men. We would fan out to spread the word and find others to help soon, but this formed a good squad. Gnaeus did not disappoint. He surveyed the stock of tools and old army weaponry, gritted his teeth, and handed them out—six Spanish swords to the most able-bodied among us, three fishing spears, a pruning hook, and two hoes. He detailed the two youths to gather the other potential weapons and carry them to the garden in the courtyard and ordered the litter bearers to look for spare planking to begin barricading the windows.

As the others set about their tasks, Gnaeus caught me by the shoulder.

"Here," he said. He reached into his army cloak and pulled out a pugio, the wasp-waisted army dagger. It was the weapon used to kill Julius Caesar a year before. I hefted the dagger in its sheath and drew it. "In the fight to come that will do more good than a sword, even our short swords. I keep it well sharpened. You can punch through a ribcage with it. At least, I have."

I looked at him and he grinned his veteran's grin. I thanked him.

"Now to tell Marcus Tullius," I said.

We returned to his door and, this time, I did not even knock. I barged in and stopped, frozen.

My old master lay still in his bed as he had before, his toga drawn up over his face as before. But now the windowsill stood lined with crows, watching. They cocked their heads at me, blinked, and resettled themselves above my master's bed. I heard Gnaeus utter a curse and back out the door behind me. My face turned to ice. Then, as I watched, one crow turned an eye down upon my master, cawed, and hopped onto the bed.

I watched for a long time. The crow hopped back and forth across the bedframe above my master's head and finally—after seeming to consider it—hopped again onto my master's pillow. It plucked at his toga, squawked, and plucked again. It flapped over his head, pecked again, caught a fold of the cloth, and began to tug in small quick movements. It drew the toga bit by bit away from his face. The other crows shuffled and squawked and bobbed their heads like so many senators listening to a speech. The crow stopped and turned its head, as if it could read my thoughts. I stepped into the room.

The crows scattered, swarmed out the window. Behind me,

I heard a gasp. I turned as I walked up to my master's bedside—it seemed the entire household had crowded into the corridor outside, goggle-eyed.

"Tell the men to forget the barricades," I said to Gnaeus, and with one hand took Marcus's Tullius's shoulder and gently shook him. His eyes opened and fixed on me.

"Leonidas?" Gnaeus said.

"Wake up, Senator," I said. "We are taking you from this place."

He looked me in the eye for some time, already awake and aware, reading me. He heaved himself upright and, after a moment, nodded. Outside, in the waning light, a crow called once and fell silent.

*

FOR THE SPACE OF HALF AN HOUR, THE HOUSE WAS IN AN uproar. Everything was upset, as Clementia had said several times that day. I ordered the litter bearers to abandon their barricading and prepare Marcus Tullius's sedan chair. One of Acte's grandsons, after I had asked which was fleetest of foot, I sent into Formiae to find the ship's captain and tell him, on my orders, to prepare the ship. The others I ordered to set the house

71

in order, leaving much of the baggage we had carried up this morning. I had them bring out the two amphorae of wine and leave them in the entryway to distract or delay any soldiers who entered there. Clementia and the kitchen slaves I ordered to prepare the modest supper usual when they had the house to themselves, and Gesataia I had bring our master what food they had ready for him to eat. Even he I gave an order: "Eat well, sir. We have a long trip ahead."

It was a plate of leftovers—mostly fish—that Clementia had set aside for me. Gesataia had supplemented it with half a loaf of dark bread and some oil. Marcus Tullius took it, thanked her, and began to eat.

"Leonidas Imperator," he said, and chuckled. "Where will you take me?"

Gnaeus and I exchanged a look, and I decided. "Greece," I said. "By way of Brindisium."

He nodded. "A trip I have made before."

I remembered—his exile during the consulship of Clodius, when all his property but this house had been burned. He had been able to return not long after the exile, but spent years setting his affairs in order. Clodius, for his part, had eventually met his end in a gang brawl on the Appian Way, a fitting end for a demagogue. His wife, Fulvia, was now married to Marcus

Antonius. Some said she controlled him. Some problems will not go away.

I told him what Acte and Gesataia had seen in town—the centurion Herennius and the tribune Popillius Laenas.

"Laenas you say," he said. "A former client of mine."

"Oh?"

"Defense case. Parricide. He murdered his father." I thought of the stories Germanicus had brought us earlier, of fathers handed over for death by their sons. I shivered. "A difficult case but he was acquitted. That was some years ago, about the time we acquired you, Leonidas."

I had thought the name Laenas sounded familiar. I told him moreover about Philologus and the two soldiers talking at a cobbler's, and Acte's suspicions. He laughed. "The cobbler! That would be Bantius Vorax, one of Clodius's old henchmen. A foul character. I am unsurprised to find him in Antonius's camp."

"Clodius," I said. "Some problems really will not go away."

"We will leave it behind soon enough," Gnaeus said. "The dead Clodius, the living Antonius, the whole lot. You can join Brutus and your son. We may yet repair the Republic."

My old master reached up with his left hand as he chewed

but, instead of resting his chin in his palm, bored, he stroked his jaw. His brows lowered almost to the point of obscuring his eyes. He swallowed a bite and spoke.

"'Repair the Republic.' Repair. I can almost smell the battlefield in your words, Gnaeus Mucius. How often have you spoken of repair while with the army—building and maintaining a bridge, mending and maintaining roads, breaching and then rebuilding and then maintaining the enemy's walls? Or, perhaps, when binding a comrade's wounds? With the exception of your comrade, these are simple and unmysterious things. Even the principles that hold an aqueduct or bridge in place in the sky or at the center of a rushing river are unmysterious, mere machines compared with the working of a man's body. How many quacks have you seen paid a soldier's lifetime wages to fail to heal a rich old woman? How many people, so distraught at the workings of their own bodies, have you seen go to quacks?

"Now, how much more mysterious is the Republic, which brings hundreds of thousands of men together in every station and walk of life, from slave and barbarian to aged censor? Think of the men that have come under this roof alone in this single day. If we approach medicine fearfully how much more so should we approach politics. But you have all listened in the baths and barber shops and now how people actually talk politics. But no—it is no simple thing to speak of 'repairing' the Republic like a machine. I've toured the army camps with Quintus who knows how often, and seen the onagers—the catapults and other engines there. You will know them intimately, Gnaeus. Well, should one fail to fling its stone or spear, one inspects it. To repair a thing one must know what is wrong with it and from what state it has descended into disrepair. You must glimpse the purpose of the thing—what Aristotle and the Greeks call the *telos*—designed into it from the beginning, and work with the same purpose as the designer. If you find then that it has a broken or missing part, you repair it or supply a new one and the machine is right again.

"So what has gone wrong with our Republic?

"No need to go back to the design—you have all heard me talk about the purpose of the Republic often enough, eh, Leonidas? How often has your hand ached with the word when taking dictation? Since we all know the purpose, what has gone wrong? What part is missing, and can we supply it? Gnaeus, when one of your onagers quits on you, you reflect back on when it stopped working, yes?"

"Of course."

"Our fathers built the Republic—this 'public thing,' a word

we have used so often we have forgotten what we are saying—out of the parts available to them. The discipline and endurance of the farmer, and piety were among them, surely. The former two made the life of the farm and war to defend family and hearth bearable. The latter ensured respect among this band of tough rustics, inured to hardship—respect for each other, respect for family, respect for the gods. They had few names for the gods back then, before the love affair with all things Greek, whether good or bad, but they had a name for the traits that held them together—virtue.

"One word to them has disintegrated into so many for us. It was a powerful word, not just the mere 'manliness' of a warrior or the 'excellence' worshiped by the Greeks, but encompassing the dignity of a man learned in the hard school of experience, the weight of such a man's opinion, his standing before others, his respect for those relationships and the respect to keep them in good repair—if you will pardon my abusing your initial metaphor, Gnaeus. This virtue and respect exalted the old Romans man by man and family by family until they—more importantly for us—grew beyond men and families into the public thing."

I thought of my reflection on Cato's family earlier. Even a family could be short-lived in comparison to the Republic. My master went on. His pace quickened—he may have said nothing when the opportunity arose on the ship that morning, but this moment he owned as his.

"These virtues, of which all men had some but did not belong to any one man, made the Republic great. It ensured its strength, its success, its endurance through so many failures and losses. Think of how many fathers willingly left their farms to face death, and think now how many defeats and slaughters the Republic had. But discipline and endurance and piety won out, and for every ten defeats the final battle brought victory. So virtue ensured success, and success brought ruin. We learned to prize beauty, and so pleasure, and so license. The farm could not offer the pleasures and rewards of the city, much less the colony. War was not defense but enrichment. Leadership was no longer a pious duty but a chance to make money. The best class clawed greedily after riches and offices, and the people, aching with their appetites, clamored for leaders who would cater to their lusts. The best class and the people—you have already heard me damn them both today. And so virtue weakened under its own rewards. Our soldiers are not even citizen soldiers any more, but state-equipped, paid professionals! What a snake we nurse in our bosom. Look what happened to Greece when flooded with mercenaries—" He stopped himself and looked at Gnaeus. "No offense intended."

Gnaeus just laughed, and I thought of our earlier conversation about his ancestors. I laughed with him. My master went on.

"Someone might object that men have always been like us, that there was greed, effeminacy, and corruption from the foundation of the city, and I would point to proportion. Men so easily forget Nature and Reason, yes, and this is a constant inclination, and so far I agree with the objection. But in some places virtue is made easy and in others hard, and in Rome the former become the latter. You can see it in our leaders. Think of Cincinnatus, respected enough to be offered the dictatorship in a crisis, respectful enough to give it up when the crisis had passed. That is virtue. I think I can stop with this one example—no need to contrast him with recent dictators."

We laughed. My master smiled, pleased with himself. No connoisseur of rhetoric ever savored an insult or insinuation more.

"No," he said, "with regard to virtue—and since he is somehow gracing us with his influence despite being deservedly dead—what about Clodius? Even beyond my disputes with him, and the exile and the politicking, think of his first great sacrilege. He dressed as a woman and snuck into the rites of the Good

Goddess, hallowed for women only since time immemorial. And not only intruding on such a rite like the hunter spying on Diana, doing so for the base purpose of seducing the hostess! Yet even though the scandal came immediately to light—who would have been fooled by such an ugly woman?—he could only be brought up on charges of incest. And then not only did Clodius find people willing to rationalize his behavior, but outright defenders. Everything culminated in Crassus, rich old Crassus himself, bribing the jury for an acquittal, and Clodius emerging more powerful and popular among the masses. Cincinnatus would have had none to listen to him should he have been involved in the prosecution. And Clodius probably would have had his houses seized, too. Ha!"

He thought for a moment, and his face brightened. "Do you recall, Leonidas, who the hostess of the rite that evening was?"

"I'm sorry, sir," I said. "That was before my time. I may not even have been born."

"No, you're right—I apologize. You see I am aging in more ways than even you have noticed. It was Pompeia—Julius Caesar's wife. He divorced her with some quip about needing a wife above suspicion, though arousing suspicions never much bothered him. Every woman's husband and every man's wife, if you remember the jibe. What does that alone say about his virtue? Or that he could let his respect for himself and his love of glory outstrip his respect of the Republic? And what of the Republic whose populace could rally to him and chase his enemies out of town? To whom would Cincinnatus have gone to complain?"

"Perhaps yourself, Senator," Gnaeus said.

He chuckled. "Now we come to my failings. Vain and proud, and vain and proud about being able to admit it. Not much of a soldier or farmer. But I have tried to grow the Old Romans' virtues as much as I could. That it takes effort is a sign of the times.

"My greatest failing, the one that has led me here, is that I tried to make peace with the times. Not like Cato, who—if you'll pardon my shushing earlier, Leonidas—contrary to Nature but in full accord with his Republican principle, died rather than submit to a tyrant. My position was confused. Near the end, with Caesar triumphant, I was undone with grief. I treasure that thing the Old Romans treasured above all, the family, and my Tullia was the dearest part of it. She joked once, she accused me of impiety for favoring her above the rest of the household, and I laughed. But perhaps it was true. Another fault. With her gone, I tried to retake my place in the Republic and save it from Julius Caesar. I cannot describe the shock of seeing him cut down like a beast, or the pleasure that mingled with it afterward. There was a chance, if we but rid ourselves of Marcus Antonius, too, Julius Caesar's henchman. And this boy, young Caesar, adopted posthumously, offered us a chance, a counterweight. Pit this strong name against that strong man, and repair the Republic. And so I befriended young Caesar, and tried to create in him the resolve to bring down Antonius. And now both have turned on me, and you drag along behind this vain old man as he tries to save himself.

"No. What made this Republic great was virtue, not any one man. How then can we trust one man to repair the Republic's greatness? Will it not change into something else? Perhaps slowly at first, and gently depending on the nature of the man—and how often are great men good men?—but change it will, and in the end be unrecognizable. The original parts have gone missing and cannot be replaced. We began building the new machine long ago, when we changed ourselves."

We sat in silence. He had, somewhere in the discussion, finished his meal, but he spoke with such feeling and dignity that we had not noticed. He sighed, content, swept his thumb around the inside of the bowl, and licked it.

"I have no peroration, if that's what you're waiting for."

We laughed. It was a mournful sound.

I looked at him sitting there on the edge of his unmade bed and, suddenly, wanted to encourage him, a client bringing a gift for the patron. I offered, "Gnaeus said to me earlier, Senator, that you as a new man are more an Old Roman than many members of the old families are today."

"Humbug. But thank you."

"That's only half the truth," Gnaeus said. "I said you and Leonidas here have that in common. Better Romans than the old families produce now."

He searched our faces, thinking. "Why do you think that is?"

"New blood," Gnaeus said.

"Leonidas?"

I had nothing. Gnaeus had just compared me to my master and, by extension, to Cincinnatus—to my master's face. "Perhaps," I said, "an attraction to what placed the current generation in its position? Even if undeserved?"

"And now the current generation threatens to unmake anyone who wishes simply to live the way that made their success."

I said nothing. I felt the danger that Clementia had spoken of again, the danger of losing all.

He looked away. "Hm. Call me Spintharus for dictation. A

letter to Atticus."

At that moment Spintharus himself leaned in, followed by one of the litter bearers.

"Everything is ready, Leonidas. Sir."

"There's no time," I said. "You can dictate to me aboard ship, or when we stop. Neapolis, maybe."

"Too many eyes and ears," Gnaeus said. "Smaller town. Herculaneum."

"Fine," I said. "Are you ready, Senator?"

He stood, pulled unashamedly at his seizing finger, and forced his fist into his hip. "Of course, Leonidas." And as he passed me at the door, "Thank you."

We left never to return, his sparse bedroom a rostrum worthy of the Forum but never to be used again. There, disheveled and long-haired, after two interrupted naps and over a plate of leftover fish, Marcus Tullius Cicero had delivered his final speech.

*

WE BROUGHT HIM THROUGH THE HOUSE TO THE ENTRY hall, where he stopped a moment at the shrine, put a rind of bread on the altar, and then took up again the figurine of his daughter before moving on. Outside the sun slid against the edge of the sea and the front of the house, the yard, all the rough hill country lay under golden light. The litter bearers waited at the door with the sedan chair. The baggage men stood around, mostly unburdened, although I saw one or two that had gathered some essential for the journey. And, I saw, all were armed.

As I ushered Marcus Tullius to his chair he reached into his toga and produced his figurine of Tullia and the sheaf of closely-written papyri—her letters.

"I realize the time is short, but please place these in the library." I reached for the letters and figurine but he held the figurine back. "All her other letters are there."

I nodded but could say nothing. Every form of excitement was upon me. I took the letters and bounded into the house. Clementia met me in the entry hall.

"What do we do now?" she said.

"Come with me," I said.

She had to trot to keep up as I went through the house to the library, deposited the letters in a carefully stacked trove with many others, and hastened back through the house.

"We have no idea where or how long or how many Antonius's men may be, so we must be quick. Down the hill to

84

the harbor as quickly as possible so they don't meet us on the road."

"Leonidas—"

Already back in the entry hall, I stopped and took her by the shoulders. "Don't be caught here."

She looked at me. "How can you talk so freely of duty to our master and not allow me to do mine?" I stared, and she went on. "I am known in the town. If I am absent after dark, something must be amiss. My duty in saving him is to help with this ruse."

I shook my head. I thought of what Gnaeus said, about non-Romans nowadays making better Romans. I thought of Marcus Tullius's speech. I pulled her into an embrace.

"They may come at any moment. Once they have searched the house, flee. Come down to the bay where the ship is beached. Go straight down along the hidden lane—" I stepped back. "The lane!"

She looked at me, puzzled. I kissed her. "Go down the lane, across the Appian Way, and straight to the sea," I said. "Turn right and you will find our ship. We will wait for you," and dashed outside.

The sun had set but the sky still glowed in ripples like a pot of molten gold in the smith's workshop. On a dark finger jutting into the deep red sea I saw the small outline of Apollo's temple, from whence the first omen had flown this morning. Was it still the same day? I thought, as I leaned into my old master's chair, that perhaps Apollo had protected him here for the day. With the god's chariot gone now, what might happen?

Marcus Tullius looked up from his book when I looked in on him. He had been reading in the last light of the gloaming. Perhaps that explained his eyesight.

"Change of plans, sir. We go by the shaded lane on the back side of the house."

"Is that not a longer path?"

"Yes, sir, but one cannot see it from the house. Especially not in the failing light."

"Good idea, Leonidas. As you wish."

Gnaeus had overheard. He stood now with his sword worn openly on his hip, his cloak flung back despite the descending night chill. "If you know this path, lead us. I'll take your place on the litter."

"No need," I said. "We all know the path, right?"

The litter bearers grunted assent. Far off, I heard a horse whinny and a curse, muffled by the distance.

"Hecate and Dis take them," Gnaeus said.

"Once down the hill," I said, "we cross the highway and

make our way down to the water. Let's go!" I stepped to my place on the carrying poles—at my master's right, just behind him. We heaved and lifted as one and turned from the main path for the back of the house to carry him to freedom. As we passed the house, I stole a glance at the kitchen windows in hopes of seeing Clementia there. The windows were dark, with no one to be seen.

We passed the house and the herb garden and the small poor vineyard and crested the top of the path. It was steep in some places and wound aimlessly down the hill, but it lay invisible from above because of the great firs and stone pines that grew along its length. In some places the path ran almost horizontally in a gallery of the umbrella pines, their branches arched overhead in a canopy and their trunks formed columns in a natural basilica, a woodland version of the courthouses where my master had spent so many days. Now, we entered at night.

The moon was already well up and its cold light taking over from the last gold of the sunset. The path, steep here at the top, lay a treacherous tangle of light and shadow. We made our way deliberately, and I understood the Gaulish girl's panic and rage against slowness at a time like this. We took some minutes in going over the first hundred yards or so, with our master shifting—without complaining—left and right in the chair with every heave of the litter bearers. I broke a sweat almost instantly, hot under my clothes and chilly on my forearms and across my face and neck. We said nothing. At last, we reached a level place, and the eight of us—with Gnaeus at our side like the centurion he was and the rest of the retinue following behind—stepped into a trot.

At that moment, we heard a shout and a girl's scream from the villa. We did not stop, even as other harsh voices joined in, growing ever more distant and faint as the trees swept by and a night breeze rustled their branches. I thought of Clementia, gritted my teeth, and willed the chair forward. When we reached the next hard turn in the path—a steeply angled switchback, the last before we would come to the Appian Way below—we saw the flames.

"They have fired the house!" one of the litter bearers cried.

"No matter," I grunted, and heard Marcus Tullius assent.

I looked up as we worked our way over the steep part of the turn. What must he have felt, watching this house burn? The others he had not even seen. Even though far off now, we could see the flames taking over the house like another sunset, and small and great shadows moving back and forth across the light. Soldiers and horses. I thought of Clementia, prayed she had escaped, and then thought of my master's library—of the letters from his daughter I had placed there—and suddenly filled with rage.

Gnaeus stood at my side and assisted with the chair in this difficult place. As if divining my thoughts he said, "We'll pay them back when we've joined with Brutus."

We left the turn and came into a long, level stretch, roofed and columned like a basilica, as I have described. It was one of Clementia's and my old private spots. We may have moved at our old trot, or may have even slowed from fatigue—I cannot now know for sure—but it felt like we sprinted. The long hall swept past in the cold moonlight and I almost fancied the sounds of hoofbeats or heavy, pounding tread behind us, driving us.

"Almost to the highway," I said to everyone and to no one in particular. "Then down to the strand and out to sea."

And in a calm voice, Marcus Tullius said, "I am afraid, friend Leonidas, that that is not to be."

I started to look up at him but my eyes caught on a black figure in the path ahead—tall, armored, wearing a crested helmet. He carried a drawn sword. For half a moment I thought we had stumbled upon Mars himself, coming to wish my master well in the fight ahead. Without a word or command, we stopped. The man ahead shifted his weight, paused, and strode toward us. Again, in silence, we set down the chair and spread outward and ahead. I felt rather than saw the men producing their weapons. The baggage men at the rear dropped their loads and fanned out in a second rank behind us. The armed man stopped, raised a hand next to his mouth, and shouted up the hill.

"Centurions at the rear! To the front!"

I heard shuffling behind me. The baggage men, weapons held inexpertly before them, peered into the darkness. We heard but did not see more men, the clatter of weapons and armor. I looked ahead again just in time to see three more soldiers appear from the brush uphill and fall into line next to the man in the crested helmet. They consulted briefly together and advanced on the chair.

"I am stopping here," I heard my master say. "Once more—save yourselves, friends. You have done all you can."

At that, most of the baggage men and some of the litter bearers looked at him, at me, at each other, and melted into the night. A handful lingered in attitudes of hesitation. Gnaeus stayed, hand on his hilt, and I found myself stepping backward to my post—just behind Marcus Tullius, and to his right. I felt the dagger at my hip and watched the soldiers come.

Behind me, a voice said, "Here, Herennius."

I turned a saw an officer in arms, his hand raised toward the centurion to the front. He too had three men. We were surrounded. I looked at my master.

Marcus Tullius sat in his chair, his chin cradled in his left palm, and watched the men approach with his face set in a mood of what I at first thought his old damning boredom. But I looked again, once more, and saw there something else—pity. He sensed me looking, glanced up at me, and nodded. Something in his look made me take my hand from the hilt of the dagger. I shook my head, and he turned back to the path. The centurion Herennius had arrived.

"No need for trouble, Gnaeus Mucius," he said.

Gnaeus said nothing, did nothing. His hand tightened on the hilt of his sword until it trembled. I swallowed and felt cold all over.

Behind me, more soldiers arrived, some staggering, tipsy, and the tribune Popillius Laenas said, "We have orders. We have no quarrel with a veteran of the legions."

Then Gnaeus looked not at them, or at the other soldiers, but at my master in his chair, and I saw then in the moonlight tears glinting in his eyes. He looked at Marcus Tullius for some time, and then, like me, lowered his hand from his weapon. Marcus Antonius's men closed in around the chair.

They smelled of leather, sweat, wine, and smoke. I saw that

their faces had darkened not in shadow but with the soot of my master's house. The centurion Herennius, who had stopped us and bluffed us into giving up our advantage in numbers, stepped in close with his sword. He peered into the sedan chair, where Marcus Tullius sat watching him, the Greek play still partially unscrolled on his lap. After a long moment, Herennius straightened.

"It's him."

I looked at Laenas. He nodded and jerked his head at the chair as if to say Get on with it. I looked at Herennius, who understood, nodded, and then looked at my master and swallowed. I blinked and understood—these men were afraid. The centurion trembled and balked. Laenas refused to come from behind the chair so that my master could see and identify him, the ungrateful client, the parricide, the emblem of the times. None of the other soldiers in the meantime would step any closer—they had busied themselves with looting the baggage and ignored us. Herennius looked at them, at me even, to steel himself, and at last his sword came up in a long practiced and now unbidden gesture.

"Oh, come now," my master said to him. "What if you had come for me first?"

Herennius gawped at him. The sword shook and the

centurion tightened his grip on it. I understood then that this was, indeed, his first execution.

"Do it," Laenas said.

Marcus Tullius lifted his chin from his palm and placed the scroll untidily back in its case. He shifted in his seat, the hip troubling him one last time, and leaned partway out of the chair into the moonlight. Without sigh or groan, he lifted his chin and with his hands—I could see the troublesome finger curled into his right palm—drew back the toga and tunic from his neck.

"You are not doing a good thing," he said. "Just make sure you do it well."

Herennius shouldered me away from the corner of the chair, put a steadying hand on my master's head, brought the edge of his sword up under the outstretched throat, and moved to slash. I turned away.

At sacrifice the priests first stun the bull with axe or mallet to render it passive before the knife. My master went dignified and in control of himself to his death, accepting Fate with the command of Reason, a willing sacrifice for the Republic. But while I stood barely a foot away as Herennius first cut his throat, then hacked once, twice, and a third time at his neck before getting down and chipping and sawing with his sword, I thought that the Republic was a small thing for so great a sacrifice. The Republic, of which my master had foretold the end, was undeserving. Nothing could be worth so much, unless it were an end to this kind of thing—to civil wars and avarice and jealousies, to widows, orphans, and masterless households, to destruction, violence, and death. Perhaps then might a good man's life be worth giving. For the Republic, such a death could be only tragedy.

*

I STOOD AND LISTENED, MY HEAD IN MY HANDS, AS THEY mangled my old master's body, as the soldiers went through the few belongings he had with him, as their leader idly watched the murder. It felt like I stood there half the night. At some point in Herennius's butchery Laenas approached me, reached for my belt—watching, cautious—and took my dagger. I looked him briefly in the face. He showed nothing.

At length I heard a curse and a thump. Herennius grunted, stood, and walked past me carrying my master's head by his untrimmed hair. I would not look at it. Laenas gestured to the chair with my dagger.

"The hands, you stupid bastard."

94

"You do it," Herennius said. "You're so eager for reward."

"Antonius's orders."

The centurion groaned and dropped his burden in a sack held by one of the other soldiers. He paused to wipe his hands and I looked back at the litter.

The body had slipped back into the shelter of the chair, the right hand draped over the side. It could have been my master reclining in the shade during a late afternoon country walk, had the side of the chair not been soaked and glittering with blood, turned a tyrant's purple in the moonlight. A puddle with outflung jets of black stood in the dust at the side of the chair, near where I would have crouched to lift the pole.

Herennius passed me, grasped the one visible hand, and jerked the arm outward over the edge of the chair. He raised his sword and aimed.

"No!"

Herennius stopped. The soldiers looked at me, the only pause in their looting. It took me some time to realize I had shouted. I swallowed and stepped up to the centurion.

"A moment, please," I said, and the centurion stepped back.

I took my old master's hand, already grown cold and waxy like the ancestor masks in any noble family's foyer, and grasped the middle finger, seized once and for all. I gave it a jerk and it popped out straight, ranked with the other fingers that I had so often seen gesture and pose. I lowered it to the edge of the chair and reached into the darkness inside. I took the scroll of *Medea* and, without looking, felt inside my master's toga. It was lukewarm and sticky and I wanted to recoil, but did not until I had found the figurine of Tullia. I took these two objects and stepped back. I said nothing. Herennius watched me and, after a moment, went back to work.

"Let me see," Laenas said.

"Bugger with Dis," Gnaeus said, and I started.

Laenas pointed the dagger at him and raised his eyebrows. He held a hand out to me. I handed over the items and he looked at them. He dropped the figurine in the dust and dumped the scroll out of its case, then ran his fingers along the inside. He looked at me and dropped the case.

"Slaves will take anything," he said.

"Done," Herennius said. He tossed my master's hands to the soldier with the bag and all at once the band moved off. Laenas took the bag and looked at Gnaeus as he passed.

"Do not let me see you again," he said.

"Likewise," Gnaeus said.

Herennius called up into the trees and more soldiers came down from the brightly glowing hilltop, a few leading horses, carrying off my master's wine, or staggering under the weight of loot or drink. They did not even take the lane, but drifted across like shades and continued down the wooded slope to the highway and thence to Rome, where Marcus Antonius would laugh over my master's head at supper and heap riches upon Laenas, where Fulvia would desecrate his noble tongue with her golden hairpins, and where my master's head and hands, nailed high for all to see, would disgrace the rostrum he had once graced with his words, hanging long enough to see Antonius and Laenas and Fulvia all dead and their laurel-crowned statues torn down and young Caesar left alone to command an Empire, but not a Republic.

The soldiers gone, the tree-columned path stood silent. We stood or sat around the bloody chair in the path and wept. I bent and gathered my master's things. The play I brushed off, then properly rolled and stowed in its case. The figurine of Tullia cleaned with great care, and took from the pouch on my belt a strip of cloth in which to wrap it. I had just finished doing so when I saw another dark figure on the path ahead, and jumped. I need not have been frightened—it was Clementia.

As others emerged from hiding—the litter bearers, the baggage men, Spintharus bloody-mouthed, Acte led by her grandsons, the Gaulish girl weeping and half-naked—

Clementia came to me like a vision out of the foggy northern marshlands. Her eyes glowed in a soot-smirched and swollen face. Her hair, silver-white in the night, hung disheveled but never more beautiful—she was alive.

I found myself sobbing. "They killed him."

She nodded and took my hand and the figurine in hers. Gnaeus joined us, and we walked down the path to the sea.

*   *   *

*   *   *

excerpt, Proceedings of the Senate and People of Rome, 30 BC:

In the matter of the petition for citizenship, with reference to documentation provided and in the judgment of the magistrate, let it be known that official recognition of freedman status and full citizenship with right of commerce, right of marriage, right of suffrage, and right of seeking office are accorded to the aforesaid freedman M. Tullius Leonidas of Antium, husband of the freedwoman Clementia, and to his sons in perpetuity.

With gratitude, by command of M. Tullius Cicero the Younger,

Consul

from Plutarch's *Lives*:

A long time afterward, so I have been told, Caesar was visiting one of his daughter's sons. The boy had a book of Cicero's in his hands and, terrified of his grandfather, tried to hide it under his cloak. Caesar noticed this and, after taking the book from him, stood there and read a great part of it. He then handed it back to the young man with the words: 'A learned man, my child, a learned man and a lover of his country.'

99

AUTHOR'S NOTE

Our principal sources for the death of Cicero are Appian (*Civil Wars*, IV, 19-20) and Plutarch's *Life of Cicero*. His demeanor and final words come from Seneca the Elder (*Suasoriae*, VI, x). Cicero's faithful freedman secretary Tiro wrote a biography of his former master which is now lost, but presumably served as a source for later historians.

Cicero's life story is well told in many modern accounts, including *Roman Realities*, a survey by Finley Hooper; *From the Gracchi to Nero*, by H.H. Scullard; *Rubicon: The Last Years of the Roman Republic*, by Tom Holland; *Caesar: Life of a Colossus* and *Augustus: The First Emperor of Rome*, by Adrian Goldsworthy; *The Death of Caesar: The Story of History's Most Famous Assassination*, by Barry Strauss; and *Cicero: The Life and Times of Rome's Greatest Politician*, by Anthony Everitt.

Cicero's many, many works (28 multi-work volumes in

Harvard's Loeb Classical Library) in a variety of genres are still in print, still widely available, and still worth reading. I recommend his *Philippics* against Antony, his *Letters to Atticus*, *On Old Age*, *On Friendship*, *On the Republic*, and *On Duties*, the last philosophical work he completed before his death. The *Self-Consolation* he wrote following Tullia's death, though much admired in the ancient world, is lost.

ACKNOWLEDGEMENTS

I am indebted to Doug Stallings for pushing me to read about Cicero during college; to John Matzko, for his memorable reenactment of Cicero's death in a semester full of memorable stories from Rome; to Caroline Dunn, for her contagious enthusiasm for a lawyer when I was a student obsessed with generals; to Coyle Neal, for indulging in a rabbit trail on Cicero while recording a podcast on Roman politics, a rabbit trail that ultimately led to this novella; to my early readers Dave, Steve, Andrew, Jim, and Mike, for their time and notes; and to Sarah, for encouraging me to make the time for this project.

GLOSSARY

Appian Way – The *Via Appia*, a major Roman highway connecting Rome with Brundisium (modern Brindisi) in southeastern Italy. Named for Appius Claudius Caecus, the magistrate who began construction on the road in the fourth century BC.

augur – A priest specially trained in augury, the interpretation of the behavior of birds. The business of the Roman state did not go forward without first consulting such omens.

censor – An official position occasionally given to the two senior members of the Senate and tasked with revising the census of Roman citizens with reference to wealth and morals— hence the modern connotations of the term.

centurion – A senior enlisted man in the Roman army, in command of a "century"—a company of around one hundred men—or in some other senior leadership capacity.

Dis – A Roman god of the underworld, often equated with Pluto.

Hecate – A Greek goddess of witchcraft and necromancy.

household altar – An altar in the family shrine located in the entrance of Roman homes and dedicated to the spirits of ancestors and the family's guardian spirits.

manumission – A release from slavery.

New Man – Latin: *novus homo*. In the Republic, a man who was the first of his family line to hold one of the magisterial offices in Roman politics and therefore a seat in the Senate.

onager– A form of catapult used as a siege engine by the Roman army.

proscription – A list of enemies to be eliminated, e.g. during the dictatorship of Sulla. Proscribed individuals, if they did not go into exile, could be killed with impunity.

pugio – A Roman army dagger with a wide, double-edged blade of six to eight inches.

ABOUT THE AUTHOR

Jordan M. Poss is native of Rabun County, Georgia. He holds
an MA in European History from Clemson University, where
he studied Anglo-Saxon England and military history. He
currently teaches history at a community college in upstate
South Carolina, where he lives with his wife and daughter. He
is also the author of the novel *No Snakes in Iceland*.